MACCABEE!
The Story of Hanukkah

For Skip, Ben, and Todd "who know what's right and do it, too" –T.B.

To my children, Chase, Nick, and Emma –D.H.

KAR-BEN PUBLISHING
A division of Lerner Publishing Group, Inc.
241 First Avenue North
Minneapolis, MN 55401 USA
1-800-4-Karben

For reading levels and more information, look up this title at www.lernerbooks.com.

Library of Congress Cataloging-in-Publication Data

Balsley, Tilda.
Maccabee! / by Tilda Balsley ; illustrated by David Harrington.
p.   cm.
ISBN 978–0–7613–4507–7 (lib. bdg. : alk. paper)
ISBN 978–0–7613–6234–0 (eBook)
1. Hanukkah—Juvenile literature. 2. Maccabees—Juvenile literature.
I. Harrington, David, 1964– II. Title.
BM695.H3B35 2010
296.4'35—dc22   2009001877

Manufactured in the United States of America
7-46087-10463-5/29/2018

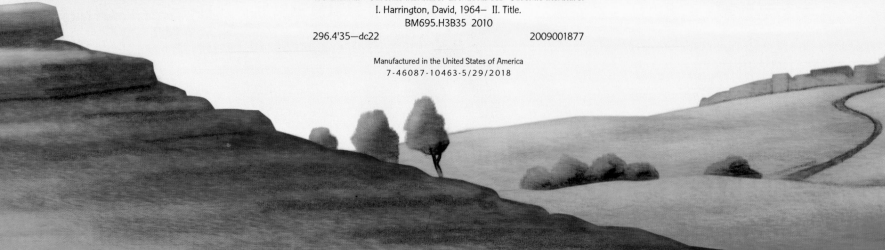

MACCABEE!
The Story of Hanukkah

Tilda Balsley

illustrated by David Harrington

KAR-BEN
PUBLISHING

At Hanukkah we tell this story
Of ancient faithfulness and glory,
Of freedom lost and freedom won,
By Jews who knew what must be done.

The Greeks had gods–yes, more than one–
God of the Sea, God of the Sun,
Throw in a Party God for fun.

King Antiochus ruled the land.
"Bow down to them!" was his command.
"And that's not all. I order you
To dress and eat and act Greek, too."
"No way," said every faithful Jew.

Sometimes it only takes a few,
Who know what's right, and do it, too.

But Antiochus had great power.
When they refused, his mood turned sour.

"Jerusalem!" He snarled and frowned.
"We'll desecrate their holy ground.
Put statues of our gods around.
Stamp out the traitors where they're found."

Some Jews gave in and some Jews fled,
Then one Jew, Mattathias, said,
"To your idols I won't pray.
Your laws aren't mine. I won't obey."
He drew his sword and got away.

Sometimes it only takes a few,
Who know what's right, and do it, too.

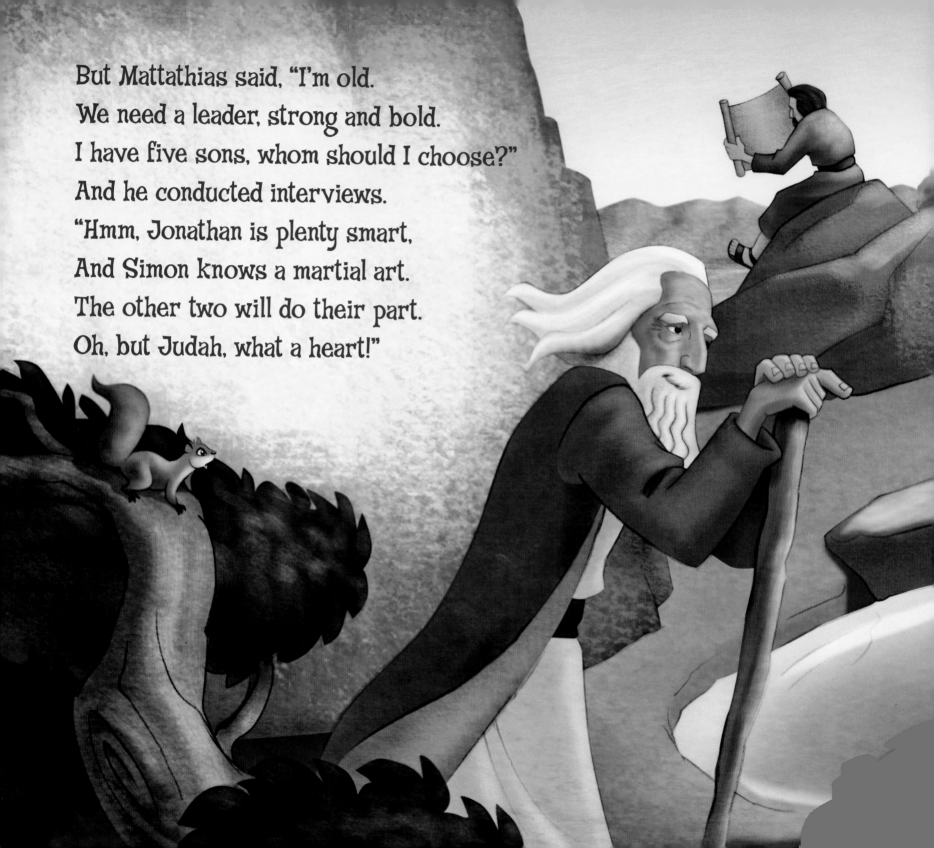

But Mattathias said, "I'm old.
We need a leader, strong and bold.
I have five sons, whom should I choose?"
And he conducted interviews.
"Hmm, Jonathan is plenty smart,
And Simon knows a martial art.
The other two will do their part.
Oh, but Judah, what a heart!"

He called to Judah at first light,
"Our farmers, shepherds, you'll unite
Deep in the mountains out of sight.
With patience, teach them how to fight,
Then lead attacks through dark of night."

Said Judah, eager, brave, and bright,
"Count on me to do what's right,
With all my heart and all my might."

Sometimes it only takes a few,
Who know what's right, and do it, too.

So Judah led the scrappy band
To fight for freedom through the land.
Now all admired his strong command,
"He's like a hammer in our hand."
So Maccabee* was his new name.
The Maccabees gained instant fame.

The armies of the king were strong.
They thought they'd win,
But they were wrong.
The Maccabees fought hard and long.

King Antiochus finally said,
"Enough, enough. Enough bloodshed."

*Maccabee derives from the Aramaic word for hammer

Then Judah's men saw just ahead—
Jerusalem—with ruin spread.
And though they'd won,
They moaned and said,
"All is lost, this place is dead."

Did Judah wail and hang his head?
No! He told them all instead,

*"Sometimes it only takes a few,
Who know what's right, and do it, too."*

"Our temple is a royal mess.
But we have come to repossess.
So do I have a volunteer
To get the idols out of here?

"I see the courtyard's gone to weeds,
Who'd like to plant some flower seeds?"

Someone called, "Look what I've found—
Our broken altar on the ground."
And Judah said, "Who's good with bricks?
These are problems we can fix."

Enthusiasm filled the air,
As people scurried everywhere.
"A new menorah—aren't we clever?
Its holy light will burn forever."

A search for oil was underway,
But bad news spoiled their holiday.
"This jug will last for just one day."

The people cried, "But it takes eight
To make more oil—and that's too late."

"You're right," said Judah, "we can't wait."
"Use what we have, that little bit."
They all agreed. The oil was lit.

The next day still it burned like new,
The third, and fourth, and fifth day, too,
For three more days, their wonder grew.

Free to worship without fear,
They said, "Remember, every year,
A miracle has happened here."
And like brave Judah, they all knew—

Sometimes it only takes a few,
Who know what's right, and do it, too.

EPILOGUE

If Judah were alive today,
What would he do, what would he say?
He'd smile at the familiar sight
Of our menorah burning bright.
And join in prayers that we recite.
He'd thrill us with a tale or two
About his brave and loyal crew.
We'd beg for more when he was through.

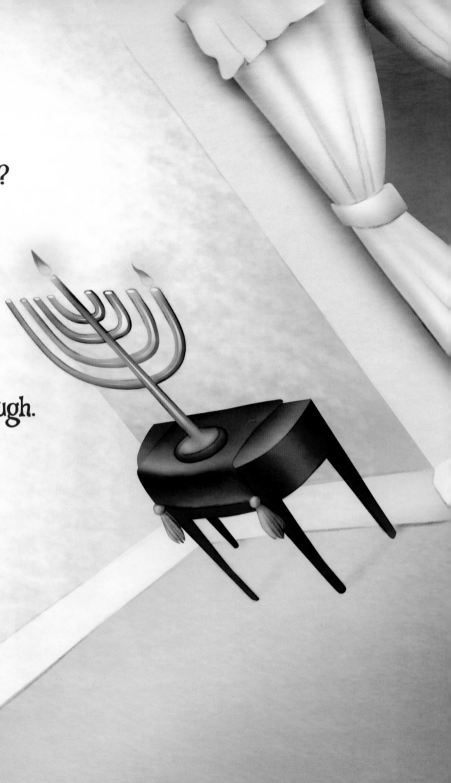

But Judah lived long, long ago.
Of course he can't come see us, so
Some of these things we'll never know.

Yet we'll remember this—it's true:
Sometimes it only takes a few.

About the Festival of Hanukkah

Hanukkah is an eight-day Festival of Lights that celebrates the victory of the Maccabees over the mighty armies of Syrian King Antiochus. According to legend, when the Maccabees came to restore the Holy Temple in Jerusalem, they found one jug of pure oil, enough to keep the menorah burning for just one day. But a miracle happened and the oil burned for eight days. On each night of the holiday, we add an additional candle to the menorah, exchange gifts, play the game of dreidel, and eat fried latkes and sufganiyot (jelly donuts) to remember this victory for religious freedom.

About the Author and Illustrator

Tilda Balsley has lived in seven states and four foreign countries. A former teacher, she loves reading and writing children's books. She is the author of *Let My People Go!*, a readers' theater story for Passover. She and her husband live in Reidsville, North Carolina, where they have raised two sons, four dogs, and a cat.

David Harrington is a graduate of California State University Fullerton with a degree in Animation and Entertainment Arts. His art has been used in TV, film, and video in addition to children's books. He lives in Fullerton, California.